P9-EEI-764

11/99

To David and Suzie, who share something special
F.W.

For Clare and Chloë
C.T.

Text copyright © 1998 by Frieda Wishinsky
Illustrations copyright © 1998 by Carol Thompson
All rights reserved.

CIP Data is available.

Published in the United States 1999 by Dutton Children's Books,
a division of Penguin Putnam Books for Young Readers,
345 Hudson Street, New York, New York 10014
http://www.penguinputnam.com/yreaders/index.htm
Originally published in Great Britain 1998 by
Transworld Publishers Ltd, London
Typography by Richard Amari
Printed in Italy   First American Edition
2 4 6 8 10 9 7 5 3 1
ISBN 0-525-46095-0

Oonga Boonga

Frieda Wishinsky ● illustrated by Carol Thompson

Dutton Children's Books ● New York

Nobody could make

Baby Louise stop crying.

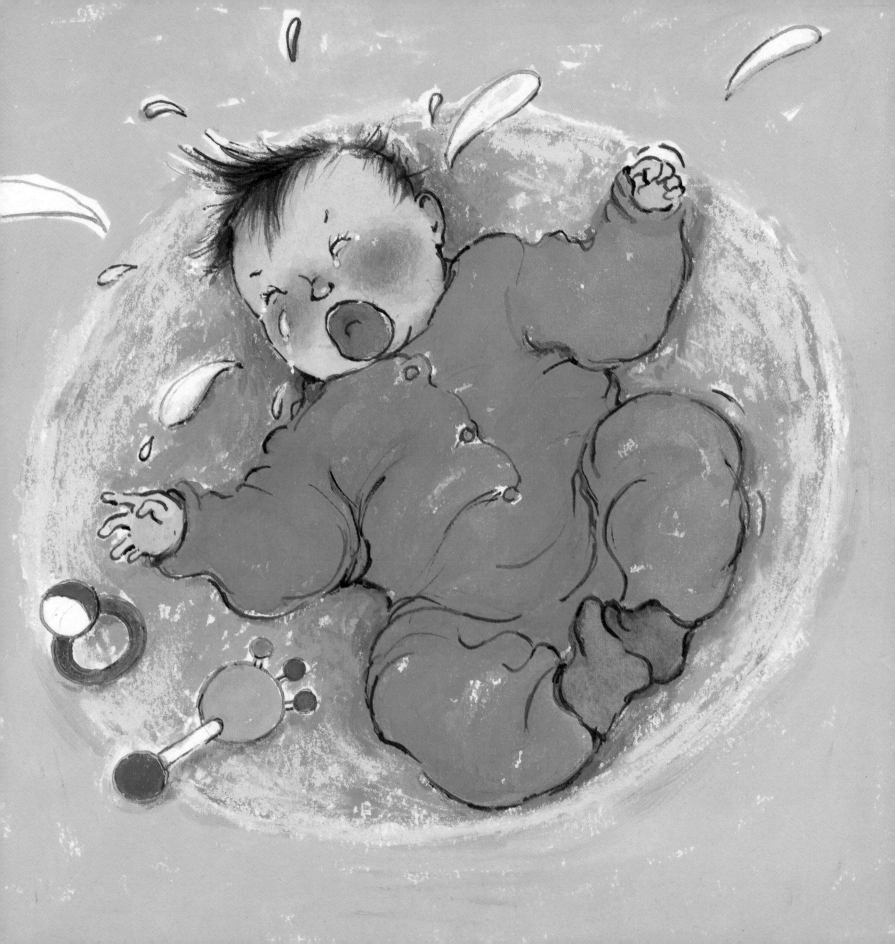

Her mother tried.

She held her close and sang a little lullaby.

But that didn't help.

Louise kept on crying until her tears ran

like rivers to the sea.

Her father tried.

He rocked her gently in his arms

and whispered softly in her ear.

But that didn't help.

Louise kept on crying until her wails

shook the pictures off the walls.

Grandma tried.

She gave her a nice warm bottle

and said, "Eat, eat."

But that didn't help.

Louise kept on crying until her sobs

woke all the dogs and cats on the block.

Grandpa tried.

He played a happy tune on his harmonica

and did a little jig.

But that didn't help.

Louise kept on crying till the birds flew out of the trees

and the squirrels scampered away.

The neighbors came and offered advice.

"Turn her on her stomach."   "Turn her on her side."

"Play Mozart."   "Play rock and roll."

But nothing helped. Louise kept on crying.

Then her brother, Daniel, came home from school.

"**Oonga boonga**," he said to Louise.

Louise looked up, tears streaming down her face.

"**Oonga boonga**," he repeated.

Louise stopped sobbing and looked him

straight in the eye.

"**Oonga boonga**," said Daniel again.

Louise broke into a smile.

"How did you do that?" asked his mother.

"It's easy. You just say **Oonga boonga**," said Daniel.

"Oonga boonga," said his mother.

"Oonga boonga," said his father.

"Oonga boonga," said Grandma and Grandpa.

"See," said Daniel. "She likes it."

And sure enough, she did.

Louise was smiling from ear to ear.

"Oonga boonga," said everyone in unison.

"I'm going out to play," said Daniel.

"Be back at six for dinner," said his mother.

But as soon as he left, Louise's smile faded.

Slowly a tear rolled down her cheek,

followed by another and then another.

And soon she was crying as loudly as before.

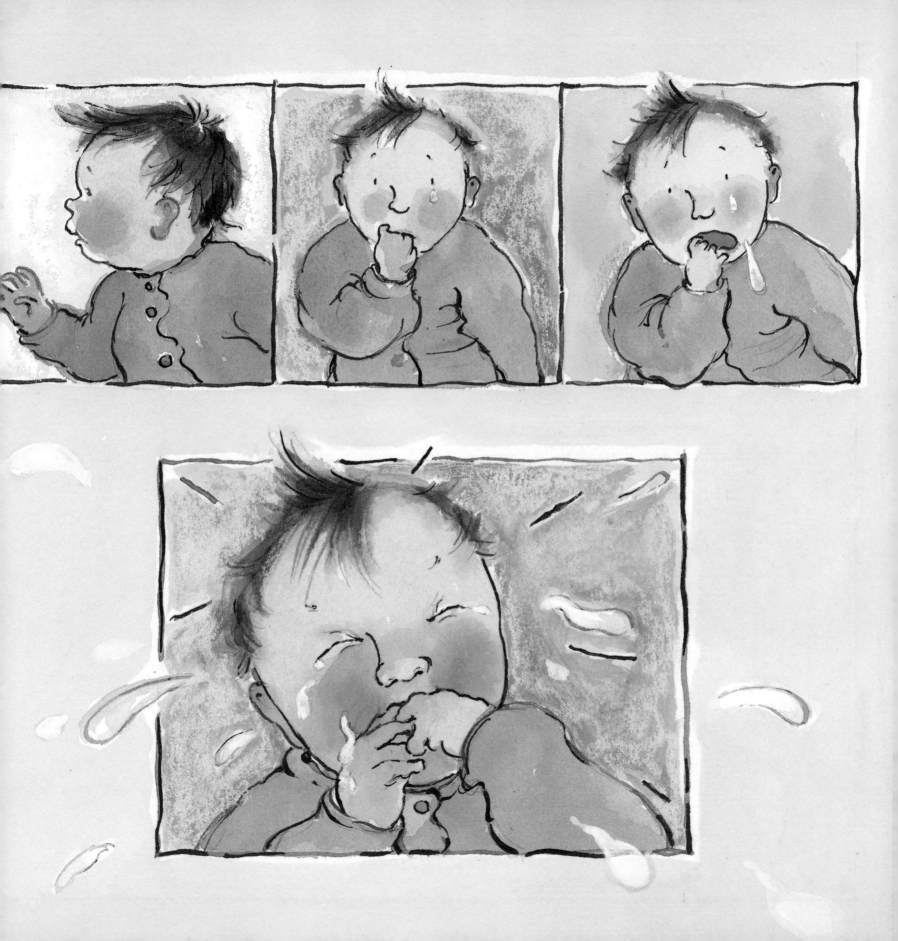

"Oonga boonga," said her mother.

"Oonga boonga," said her father.

"Oonga boonga," said Grandma and Grandpa.

But nothing helped. Louise kept on crying.

"What's wrong?" said Daniel.

"Oonga boonga doesn't work anymore," they said.

Daniel leaned over Louise

and whispered in her ear:

"**Bunka wunka**, Louise."

And Louise stopped crying.